Elves, Trolls & Cheese Curls – A Tale of Icelandic Creatures

HaiDi Pye

Merry Christmas,
Aunt Barb!

Love,
HaiDi Pye
12-25-15

DEDICATION

For Mimi, who asked for simply a short story based on my adventures in Iceland as a birthday gift, which turned into an amazing set of works written by me and four other authors, and essentially brought the fictional writing and creativity out of us all.

Happy Birthday!

CONTENTS

ACKNOWLEDGMENTS

Thank you very much to:

my aunt, **Allison Graham**, who expanded the humor of the stories with her hilarious work.

my cousin, **Zukhra Graham**, who brought family members into her work, making us all laugh and smile.

my sister, **Joy Pye,** who wrote beautifully so we could all see the scenery of where these stories take place.

my mother, **Susanna Graham-Pye**, who travelled to Iceland with me in 2013, and who used her amazing writing skills once again to please us all with her story.

my grandfather, **Thomas Graham**, who happily read aloud the ending of Book One every time before someone started their Book Two.

my grandmother, **Kathie Grenon,** who made it possible for us to write these stories for her birthday.

BOOK ONE: THE BEGINNING

ONCE UPON A TIME, there lived an elf named Adam who lived in Selfoss, Iceland. For the most part, he was like any other elf, he caused mischief and during the day when the sun was out, hid in the rocks. However, the only difference was while most of the elves were fairly short, Adam was a very tall, lanky elf. Every time he tried to run into the cave where he lived, he'd find himself bumping his head on the ceiling – every, single, time. Even though they were covered in a thick layer of green moss, it still hurt. All of the other elves made fun of him because of his un-elfy figure. He knew for a fact he wasn't human (because he was too short), but he was too tall to be an elf. Adam decided he was going to visit the famous Icelandic wizard, who knew everything. Fladnag was his name and he had a long white beard that dropped down to his knees; his cloak was just as white as his beard.

Adam waited until nightfall before heading out to find Fladnag (elves are not supposed to see the sun or else they'll turn to stone so legend had it, and he wasn't about to find out for himself if that was true - or not). Creeping into the city of Reykjavik, hiding in the shadows of buildings, Adam found himself at the tall building with glowing letters declaring "Hotel Reykjavik" on the front of it. All but the top window on the far left were dark – evidence that Fladnag was there. Rumor had it, he travelled the Rocky Roads, which was really a bike path but he convinced everyone, as well as himself, it was a sacred path that only the courageous members of society could take, but would occasionally stop by random towns and rent out an entire hotel so no humans could see him.

Adam snuck inside one of the lobby windows, for the front doors were locked tight, and was greeted by a dark narrow room, not a sound to be heard. A fancy chandelier dangled from the center of the ceiling, its crystals sparkling brightly even though there wasn't any light. Adam tiptoed through the long hallways, finding his way to the elevator. This took him no time at all, because like all the other elves, he had super night vision. Pressing number 24 on the elevator buttons, he felt himself shoot upward. In less than four seconds, he stepped out of the elevator, which snapped shut just as he left its presence, and found himself before a long hall that stretched left, and another by his right that stretched, well, in the opposite direction. Hesitantly taking a right, Adam stumbled to the very last hotel room, dragging his bare-feet against the red carpets which rolled out over the hall's floors.

The polished wooden door was marked 4999 and had a blinding light seeping out from under the door. Adam knocked on the door, but got no response. Knocking once again, louder this time, the light went out and the door swung open. A tall bearded man stood in front of him, his eyes narrowed and wiry hands wrapped tightly around his staff.

"Who are you?" hissed the wizard. He looked exactly like they said he did. "Can't you see I am in the middle of practicing my magic? Why I should turn you into a cow right now."

"Oh please, do not do that," Adam cried. "I was coming to ask you a question, and with your wisdom, oh mighty one, I may be able to find the answer. Will you please help me?"

Fladnag, the wizard sighed and rolled his eyes but finally stepped out of the way, letting Adam enter the room. "Alright, Adam, how can I help thou?" he demanded, sitting down on a plush sofa, which was covered with feathery black and white pillows. "Sit. Tell me your story."

Adam sat on the edge of his own chair, ready to jump up and run if he angered Fladnag. "I was raised believing I was an elf, but I am much too tall to be one, you see; and I can't be a human, because I'm too short. It's not one of those unusual cases like Buddy the elf-faced. I know for a fact, I am not human."

Ah yes, my younger brother, Santa Claus, dealt with that elf's problems," Fladnag said. "Buddy was a terrible elf, but a good human."

"You have a brother?"

"Yes. Santa Claus, he's my younger brother. Then there's Dalfgan, my twin brother. You don't want to know how old any of us are. Anyway, enough of this. Why did you think I could tell you?" Fladnag asked.

"Because. You're FLADNAG, the great and powerful, y'know?" Adam squirmed uncomfortably in his chair, wondering if visiting Fladnag was a good idea in the first place. "You…you can help me, right?" He held his breath, waiting for the disappointment to slap him in the face.

"Hmm…let me see…. Well, first off. What do you want me to do? Tell you whether or not you're an elf or something?" Adam nodded, so Fladnag continued. "Alright, let me get my Magic Ball of Knowledge." Fladnag rose, walked into the tiny kitchen, rummaged around inside the refrigerator, and came back with a crystal, glowing sphere.

"Whoa."

"Yep, that's the Magic Ball of Knowledge," Fladnag stated proudly. Dalfgan has a Magic Ball of Wisdom, but that's stupid; mine's better. So let's start, shall we?"

"Step forward, place your tiny little hand—the right one—on the top of it. Yes, like that. Good, good. Now let's see if I remember the spell…." He leafed through a giant book, leather and covered with dust, and opened up to a page yellowed with age. "Not sure what to be / lost I am / set me free / so I can be myself / define who I am / and who I must be!" Fladnag quoted from the book, dust flying as his breath hit the page. The Magic Ball of Knowledge flashed brightly, slightly ruining Adam's eyesight for a few seconds, before returning to its plain old self.

"That's it?" wondered Adam.

"Yes."

"What did that do? I feel the same. Am I taller? Or Shorter?"

"Nope." Fladnag sat down, resting the Magic Ball of Knowledge in a nest of feathery pillows beside him. "You are still the same. Unfortunately, this magic didn't work on you. It couldn't identify your species."

"Meaning…?"

"Meaning that you must be one thing. The only thing this Magic Ball of Knowledge can't identify are trolls. You must be a troll."

"A TROLL???" Adam gasped. I…why, those are beasts, monsters, they're…**trolls!**"

Fladnag chuckled, even though nothing about this was funny. "Yes, they are trolls. I understand that you elves and trolls have had a rough history, but maybe it's time you correct the conflict. You can unite them. You are the only elf-like troll capable of doing this."

"I refuse!" Adam shouted, jumping to his feet. "I am not a troll! Trolls are disgusting, huge creatures that terrorize everyone. They scare little children for fun!"

Long ago, lived a giant female of a troll named Gryla. She was a bitter troll, always eating naughty children. She was constantly hungry. One of Gryla's husbands, Leppa-Ludi, had an affair with an elf named Skjoda. Furious, Gryla cursed the elf and her entire family (her family was quite large). Skjoda and her family, as well as Leppa-Ludi, suffered slowly, day by day feeling their bodies freeze up. First, it was their feet that became stiff, soon it moved up to their knees, shoulders, and before they knew it, all of them had become stones, frozen forever. The elves all grew mad at Gryla for doing this so they formed angry mobs and attacked her. Just as she was about to die, she turned herself into stone so she could live forever. Her thirteen sons wanted to avenge her death, but all of the elves had hidden in moss-covered rocks, becoming known as the "hidden folk." The sons are still alive, some say, and they are still hunting down the hidden folk, trying to seek revenge. Every day, however, when the sun comes up, they are forced to turn into stone temporarily and begin searching again in the night. The relationship between the hidden folk and trolls had become icy and they'd been fighting against each other ever since.

"Ah, that's only because the children are naughty. Trolls rarely bother the innocent ones. Come on, they aren't that bad."

"Yes, they are. My parents, who are both **elves**, I might add, said they are. Trolls are bad, hidden folk are good," Adam argued. "We can't disobey our beliefs."

"Well you are going to have to accept your new identity," Fladnag snapped. "Now, if you don't mind, I am going to go back to practicing my magic. Please leave."

As Fladnag rose, so did Adam. "No, wait! What am I to do, sir? I can't live with the elves and be a troll! They'll hate me."

"Unite the species, Adam. That's all I can tell you. And by doing so, you must find the trolls and introduce yourself. Can you do that?"

"But, what if they chop off my head?"

"Then that'll be a shame. It's risky, but possible. Just don't get on their bad side, and you'll be fine. Now go. Now. It's the only thing you can do. Travel up to Krafla, where the hot springs, geysers and volcanoes all are. You'll find most of the troll population up there, hiding out for a while. They travel everywhere, but from what I can gather, they're there now. You only have a few weeks before they pack up and leave. "

"Alright," Adam said cautiously, "when should I leave?"

"Right now, of course." Fladnag waved his staff, and a backpack floated over to them. Inside the thin fabric, there was a pickaxe, rope, flashlight, a small gem-encrusted dagger, coils of both thick and thin wire, a couple of bottles of water and troll food (which consists of various dry meats, crackers and cheese curls).

"This is all you'll really need for your trip; it should only take one day at the most," Fladnag explained. "But it's dangerous still. Say one wrong thing to a troll, and they'll eat your brains out. Get on their good side, however, and you've got a friend for life. So, be off now."

"That's it?" Adam examined the bag's contents carefully. "I can't travel by day or else the humans will see me."

"Not only that, but because you are a troll, you'll turn to stone if the sun's rays hit you," the wizard added. "So don't be out in the sun."

"What?! You expect me to go outside after telling me that? I'll turn to stone? Oh my goodness, I'll be frozen for life!"

"Yes, that is true. So be careful. I cannot assist you, but I will use my portal to transport you to Bjarnarflag, which is south of Krafla. If you stay on the trail, you'll get there before the sun rises. They've got giant caves. I'm sure they'll welcome you in."

"Okay," Adam said confidently after a second. "I'll do it, for the good of elf kind, as well as, the trolls. They should be united, like you said. But if I die on this journey, I am totally blaming it on you."

"Fair enough," Fladnag shrugged. He tossed his staff up in the air, as if it were a baton, creating a purple circle-like portal. Fladnag stepped aside, so Adam slung the backpack onto his back, glanced back once over his shoulder, and jumped.

He felt as if his body was being stretched apart and then squashed while travelling through the portal. It was a very uncomfortable feeling, so he promised himself that he'd never do it again. Next time, he'd rather walk the extra miles.

Adam found himself standing in front of a rocky landscape, complete with numerous geysers and bright blue water. The water looked like opaque turquoise. When he let his feet slosh through the shallow water, he felt the water's perfected temperature.

Oh, if only I could waste some time and relax in these refreshing waters, Adam thought to himself. He felt steam and droplets of hot water splash onto him from a nearby geyser which erupted with a **poosh** sound. It felt magical, but Adam knew he had no time to waste. He started forward, guided by his flashlight.

The walk was pleasant, just the quiet noise of occasional geyser eruptions, and a few crickets chirping. The moonlight, along with the colorful Northern Lights, amplified his night vision helping him see after half an hour, when his flashlight flickered off. The path was easy to follow. (All trolls, hidden folk, dwarfs, and water-dwellers have a built in GPS so they can never get lost unless entering a totally different country.)

Just as the sound of the geysers faded away in the background, Adam heard footsteps following him. They were loud, clumsy footsteps, not like elves or trolls, who had soft and careful ones, so they could stay hidden from humans. But when Adam stopped, so did the footsteps. Slowly, he tiptoed forward a couple of feet, only to hear them echoed. He did it again, but this time the footsteps behind him didn't stop—they continued coming closer. In less than five seconds, a tall figure hovered over Adam, nothing but a black silhouette.

"Who are you?" the figure asked. It was a gentle voice, still pretty young sounding. "Are you an imp?"

"I am most definitely **not** an imp," Adam snarled. Imps were even worse than trolls. "I am an elf slash troll, thank you very much," he scoffed.

"Oh," the voice said. "I'm a human. My name's Freyr. I turned ten last week."

"A...**human?**" Adam gasped. He hadn't even thought to consider what kind of species this thing could be. He believed it was an ogre or something, not a **human.** "I..." Adam dug around in his backpack, pulling out the dagger. "Take one more step and I swear, I'll feed you to the trolls that I'm going to see. I heard they love tasty children like yourself."

"I am not naughty, though," the human boy named Freyr said. "My mom said only the bad kids get eaten. I am not bad."

"I'm going to have to kill you, Freyr," Adam said. He felt bad about it, but the kid had to die after seeing him. "Any last words?"

"No, wait!" Freyr cried. "I won't tell anybody I saw you. Besides, nobody believed me when I told them I saw an elf last year."

"Nobody believes? What do they think we are then?"

"Fake creatures. That you're part of stories meant to scare kids. But I knew you were real. Where are you going?"

Adam returned his dagger to his pack nervously. He believed Freyr, but still, he felt as though he should be more cautious. "I'm going to seek out the trolls. For all my life, I was told that I'm an elf, or a hidden folk. But Fladnag, the wizard, told me I was a troll. Elves and trolls don't get along. Nobody will accept me now, because I'm a troll who acts like an elf. In order to return to my home, I must unite the trolls and elves. I'm going to Krafla."

"Oh that sounds fun," Freyr chirped happily. "Can I come? Please? I won't disturb you or anything. I'll just keep you company."

"I don't know, Freye," contemplated Adam. He was lonely, but having a human as company would upset the trolls for sure. "The trolls won't like you."

"I'll leave before we get there."

"Shouldn't you be in bed?"

"Yes, but I live fairly close to Krafla, just a half an hour walk maybe and I'll be home before the sun even rises."

"Hmm."

"Pleeeease?"

"Okay, fine. But you have to leave when I'm ten minutes away from the troll cave, understand? If they find you, everything will be ruined. Also, if you tell any humans about the troll caves, or elves or anything, I'll be forced to make you keep quiet," Adam warned. "And that's not a good thing."

"I won't!" My lips are sealed." Adam nodded, and the two started walking forward. Freyr did as promised and didn't bombard Adam with annoying questions, he just followed him through the dark of the night. The trip was silent except for the tapping of footsteps; one barely making any noise, the other thumping loudly.

After fifteen minutes or so, Adam stopped suddenly. Freyr skidded to a halt as well, curiously looking around.

"What—" Freyr started to whisper.

"Hush. I hear something." Adam crouched down behind a large boulder. Freyr did the same, still confused. After a few seconds, Adam turned to Freyr, fear in his eyes. "Trolls," he mouthed. His large finger trembled as he pointed down the hill to an army of trolls marching toward them. Torches were held, creating a visible path for them. Adam and Freyr sucked in their breaths, thinking what to do.

"We could make a run for it," Freyr suggested.

"No, trolls are fast. They can also shoot arrows from miles and miles away. They've got excellent aim. Hiding is our only option." Adam started to crawl to another boulder.

"Why can't we just talk to them now?" Freyr trailed behind him.

"Because, they don't like to be disturbed during their marches. They consider them sacred, and if we bother them, they'll cook us before we can say anything." The two sat uncomfortably behind a boulder, waiting for the army to march away. But they didn't, the rows of trolls just kept coming and coming. They sang their troll chants, ate drumsticks, laughed, played with their swords....they did stuff trolls like to do.

Adam and Freyr sat in silence for what seemed like hours, and the army still hadn't stopped.

"I'm hungry," Freyr complained.

"What do you humans eat? Do you like cheese curls?"

"Mm! We love cheese curls. Do you like them?"

"Of course, everyone does," Adam said, offended. He pulled out a bag of cheese curls, curing their stomachs' hunger. Minutes passed before they ran into trouble.

A large troll, twice the size of Adam stopped suddenly and howled. Everyone else stopped, too. **"I SMELL CHEESE CURLS!"** he shouted. The crowd of trolls went crazy, leaping and hissing foam out of their mouths. "Cheese curls, cheese curls, cheese curls," they said monotonously. A small troll, whose skin was green, sniffed the air ferociously and turned his head in the direction of Adam and Freyr. **"Cheese curls,"** he growled. Racing towards them, he led nine other trolls his size over to them.

"Run!" Adam yelled. He and Freyr raced away from the army. The whole army of trolls had seen them, so they all started after them. Panting, Adam grabbed Freyr and pulled him into a cave. The trolls ran right past them without even noticing.
"That was close," Freyr gasped. His heart was pounding so loudly he could hear it echo through the cave. "Thank goodness they didn't catch us."

Just as the words left his lips, torches which lined the sides of the cave were lit, enlightening the entire cave. Hundreds and hundreds of trolls stood staring at them. In the center, a lanky troll stood with a red cape draped from his shoulders. As he walked forward, it dragged on the ground, collecting dirt.

A few feet away from the intruders, the troll spoke in a booming, gravely voice. "My name is Teitur. I am King of the Trolls. Welcome to our

9

cave."

END OF BOOK ONE

BOOK TWO – WHAT HAPPENS NEXT

Adam and Freyr started to run, but were immediately grabbed by the surrounding trolls. Rusty metal chains were wrapped tightly around their wrists, chafing their skin. The trolls erupted into laughter, which echoed throughout the cave, shaking Freyr's weak human ears with the deafening noise. It took a few seconds before the chaos came to a halt when Teitur spoke in his gravelly voice.

"Identify yourselves, beasts of Iceland," Teitur commanded. "State your reason for entering private property."

"W-well, sir…um, we have been sent by the great Fladnag," Adam stuttered. "To unite t-the trolls and elves. And—"

"Liar!" a troll yelled from within the crowd. "I bet you've never seen Fladnag in your life!"

"Silence, Olaf," Teitur said, glaring at the other troll. Turning to Adam and Freyr, he questioned them further. "So tell me, little troll and little human, why did Fladnag send you? Did he have a message for us that he was too lazy to send himself?" More laughter from the trolls, who weren't as awed by Fladnag's powers.

Gathering as much courage as he could, Adam explained himself. "Fladnag, the twin brother of Dalfgan and the older brother of Santa Claus, spoke with me not long ago. I asked him to distinguish my species. For years, I grew up thinking I was an elf, but no, I am indeed a troll."

Before the troll could reply, an orange cloud of mist appeared, staying for a few seconds before disappearing again, leaving behind a tall figure.

"I AM DALFGAN, THE DEATHSLAYER," the figure announced. "I have come to explain the truth, and nothing but the truth. My brothers are Fladnag, the Great and Santa Claus, the Cunning. We make up the Mighty Trio.

"You ignorant creatures have been bickering from before anyone can remember. You foolish trolls and elves have not known that there is a third animal kind entering Iceland. One far more powerful than ye. Humans. They are coming. And with them, machinery powerful enough to destroy your homes. If you want to be homeless and/or die, so be it. However, if you want to live, you have to unite the trolls and elves and create an army."

There was a long pause in the cave and it seemed as though everyone was holding their breath. Dalfgan addressed the awkward silence by declaring his abrupt departure. "Off I go." Dalfgan left, with the same dramatic way with which he entered, leaving the others still frozen in disbelief.

Finally, Teitur took charge, shouting out orders. "You heard the man, I want all swords, spears, shields, and longbows sharpened and brought to me immediately." Instantly, the trolls ran around gathering weapons, hidden within the cracks of the cave. In less than ten minutes, a plethora of weaponry was piled neatly before the chief troll's feet.

"What about the human?" the troll, who's name was Olaf, asked, eyeing Freyr warily. "Can we kill him?"

"Over my dead body you will," Adam said, feeling a sense of loyalty to the small boy.

"That can be arranged," Olaf sneered, coming closer.

"Enough. The boy stays alive," Teitur growled, "for now at least. I want you two"—he pointed to Freyr and Adam—"to stay out of our way until I say. We're going to form an alliance with the elves, and I don't want your annoying habits to get in our way. Is that understood?"

"Yes, sir," Adam and Freyr said in unison.

An hour later, all of the trolls had some sort of tool in their hands, and were wearing a poor attempt of armor (which was really just tin plates and cups bent to fit them properly).

"Be careful of the hidden folk, they're sneaky devils," warned Teitur as they marched out of the cave over to the elf realm. Freyr and Adam stumbled behind the fast paced creatures, struggling to keep up. The fact that they also walked beside Olaf intimidated them greatly.

They walked through the diverse scenery of Iceland, passing a mixture of natural areas, such as the moss covered rocks, hundreds of waterfalls, and glaciers. Dawn slowly rose again, its red fingers slicing into the magenta sky behind the mountains. A pair of arctic foxes pranced around, frolicking in the grassy areas.

"I was born in Greenland," Freyr said randomly. "but my family and I moved to Iceland not long ago – into Selfoss. Then we moved to Reykjavik."

Adam nodded, not knowing how to respond to the comment. He glanced around, blinded by the sun which was already halfway risen from the horizon. The simplistic scenery was overbearing for Adam, who had spent his life inside a cave for years.

The thought struck him hard. "I'm in the sunlight!" Adam screamed. "What…how…am I dead?"

"Shush, you inane dwarf," Olaf snarled. "Dalfgan placed a spell on us, to prevent the sun from turning us to stone."

Keeping quiet, Adam looked glumly down at the rocky terrain, embarrassed by his mental breakdown. The surreal landscape left Adam's mind, as a negative grudge against Olaf, the troll, formed.

"Stop here," Teitur ordered. "This is them."

"How do you know?" Freyr asked the chief troll.

"Spelunking," Teitur explained. "Years and years of exploring caves. I know an elf cave when I see one. C'mon, trolls, get your weapons ready. We're confronting our enemies."

The trolls shook the fear out of their systems. Although he was terrified, Adam tried to seem nonchalant about the whole situation, for it was his hometown. But how would they react when they found out he was really a troll?

Off the army of trolls, Adam and Freyr went, preparing themselves for the entrance into the elf realm.

"Who goes there?" a voice commanded.

And there, in the dark corners of the cave, stood the king of elves. There, stood Adam's very own father.

END OF BOOK TWO - HP

ALTERNATIVE BOOK TWO: AG

Or "A few feet away from the intruders, the troll spoke in a booming, gravelly voice. "My name is Teitur. I am King of the Trolls. Welcome to our cave."

There was a loud thump behind Adam as Freyr fainted. The fact that his fantasies were in fact true, was too much for his human mind to handle. There Adam stood alone without anything. No weapons, no magic (he had left the backpack when they ran), and no help from the human! Even his voice seemed to have disappeared.

Adam's mouth was open but no words came out - just a high-pitched whine like fingernails on a chalkboard. When he finally realized that the horrible sound was coming from him, he shut is mouth hard, biting his tongue.

The hundreds of trolls who had been clutching at their ears in agony, stood glaring at Adam, the cause of their pain. The King, whose welcoming had been spoken with kindness and warmth, now looked at Adam with icy eyes. Adam felt a chill run up his spine and he slowly started to raise his hands in what he hoped was a universal sign for SURRENDER. He was clenching his fists so tightly that his fingernails were digging into his palms, drawing blood. As he stretched his fingers above his head a drop of blood fell to the ground and an agonizingly silent moment became even more so. Adam slammed his eyes shut trying to hide in the darkness. He searched his mind for the elfin words that would that would take him to a happier place but like his voice, his brain seemed to have shut down. There was no escape. He had to face this! It was his mission. Fladnag thought he could do it!

Adam peeked through his squinched up eyelids and to his surprise no one was looking at him anymore. They were looking just above his right shoulder. He slowly turned and jumped, startled to find the King of the Trolls sniffing his hand. "Dear god!!! He smells my blood," thought Adam. He was sure he would soon be eaten. The King took hold of Adam's wrist (which Adam was still holding in the air) and slowly pulled it closer to his dripping troll teeth ....Adam couldn't watch, he slammed his eyes shut again. But instead of razor like teeth ripping away chunks of flesh, Adam felt a gentle caress on one finger. His eyes sprang open to see the King smacking and licking his lips, tipping his head back and howling.... **"CHEEEESE CURLS!!"** An avalanche of sound hit Adam as hundreds and hundreds of trolls jumped up and down squealing and clapping like toddlers in a bouncy house.

"I know where we can get more." The whisper was so close to his ear that Adam almost jumped out of his skin. It was Freyr. Adam had forgotten about the eager human and for a moment, he didn't feel quite so scared. He was also very confused.

"What are you talking about!?!?" Adam shouted.

"Look," Freyr said, as he pointed back to the trolls.

They were now dancing with each other like it was a festival of some sort. Adam suddenly realized that the thumping rhythm was actually the male trolls chanting, "CHEE, CHEE, CHEESE CURLS, CHEE, CHEE, CHEESE CURLS!"
Adam felt a smile cross his face as he realized that the trolls were not going to eat him. They wanted Cheese Curls."

"Wait!" shouted Adam.

All went still and silent except for the occasional pebble bouncing down the cave walls, loosened by all the jumping trolls. Hundreds of trolls' heads turned toward Adam. There was a loud thump, as Freyr fainted again. Lot of good that silly human was.

"We," Adam said as he pointed between Freyr (on the ground) and himself, "have more cheese curls! **AND** he (pointing at the lump on the ground) can get lots more!"

Freyr's eyes fluttered open as Adam dragged him into a sitting position in front of the king. With eyes looking like a deer in the headlights, Freyr just nodded.

Teitur, King of the Trolls, walked toward the couple, the human and .... the what?? Something was familiar but the king couldn't place it, like a melody that you can't quite hear. He loomed over Adam and Freyr, who were sure they were finally about to be eaten and said, "Show me, little friend."

Whaaat???? Adam thought. What kind of a troll was this? Maybe he had been wrong about trolls! They weren't the monsters everyone said they were!!! They were just a little grumpy from constantly having to search for their favorite treat, you guessed it .... Cheese Curls.

Adam, the troll/elf and Freyr, the human, shared their story over a bowl of cheese curls. It was the first time a human, troll and troll/elf had shared anything!!! And it was just the beginning .....

END OF BOOK TWO - AG

ALTERNATIVE BOOK TWO: ZG

Or "A few feet away from the intruders, the troll spoke in a booming, gravelly voice. "My name is Teitur. I am King of the Trolls. Welcome to our cave."

When Adam and Freyr entered the cave, they were surrounded by trolls. Adam was only scared about having another troll figure out he was part elf. Freyr was biting his nails; he had never seen so many trolls. King Teitur had made an offer to Adam and Freyr to stay for the night knowing that Adam would turn to stone. In the morning, Freyr was the first one up and then Adam, they noticed that no one was in the cave except the two of them. Adam and Freyr found a note on the table that read, "Off to find some food – be back later. We packed some stuff for your journey and a magical wand to transport you to places. Good luck. – Teitur." Adam picked up the bag of stuff and took out the wand. He had had some experience with some types of wands. Freyr noticed that the wand had four numbers. Adam pressed one of the buttons and all of a sudden, the ground began to shake, then everything went black. Both Adam and Freyr woke up to the sound of running water. Adam and Freyr noticed a couple of nearby elves, named Mimi and Thomas. Mimi and Thomas asked if Adam was an elf. Adam replied, "yes, but you mustn't tell anyone". Both, Mimi and Thomas agreed to never tell a soul. Mimi offered to help Adam and Freyr on their journey, but Thomas and Mimi didn't know that the journey was to unite the trolls and elves. Once Adam and Freyr told Mimi and Thomas the plan, they were both surprised. Adam and Freyr decided to head back to the mouth of the cave where they expected to meet King Teitur. When they got there, he was shocked that they had brought the elves with them. He thought it was a bad plan. He also didn't like the idea of uniting the trolls and the elves. He said, "you are all exiled forever from this land". Really, it was only the trolls who didn't want to unite. The elves were okay with it. So they thought – "Fine, we will just leave." The king said the trolls should follow the elves back to their lair and kill them. The elves had found out from Adam and Freyr that there was a plan to go after them. When the trolls arrived, the elves were already in hiding. The elves had secret blow guns that changed the trolls perspective when they were hit by the darts. They no longer felt the need to kill any of the elves; they, too, wanted to unite. Mimi and Thomas negotiated a contract for the elves and trolls to sign, pledging that they would no longer kill each other. They all lived happily ever after.

END OF BOOK TWO - ZG

ALTERNATIVE BOOK TWO: JP

OR "A few feet away from the intruders, the troll spoke in a booming, gravelly voice. "My name is Teitur. I am King of the Trolls. Welcome to our cave.""

The slow-rising of the early dawning sun bore a still, crisp air embellished in serene hints of silver light on high above Krafla Volcano, Iceland. Neighboring plovers dipped their slender stilts into the heat of geothermal lagoons ,rimmed with fragile rubble dispersed widely atop a canvass of dust. A radiant sensation of native majesty swept the region while inside the hidden troll lair Adam and Freyr slept soundly. With a small labored effort, Adam's eyes opened to a curious and unexpected setting. Above him, a dark bronze beam of mountainous rock formations which cascaded downward, exquisitely fashioned the ceiling. The quiet breath of the small human boy beside him was peculiarly relaxing yet reassuring of the strange array of events that had ensued the day before. Adam thought back to the blur of what had happened after finding himself trapped in the infamous cave of trolls. To both Adam's and Freyr's astonishment, Teitur was gregariously welcoming, well-tempered and kind. Teitur introduced himself as King of the Trolls, a title supposedly accompanied with words pertaining to wisdom in ancient Icelandic legend. Adam and his mortal companion were led deep into the cave while Teitur casually recounted the history of his own kind. During their cave travels each felt accepted, as they were told antiquated tales, were offered drumsticks, and requested to relate their own life stories before being shown to a secluded niche for themselves far inside the folds of the cavern.

"Rest and reflect for as long as desired," the understanding troll king instructed in his heavy, bellowing voice. Luckily Adam's unique troll eyesight aided in distinguishing things in the dark, as the torches that where embedded in the jagged wall had lost their burning, red flames hours ago. When awakening, he gradually arose to his bulky troll feet and began to work his way through the cryptic twists and turns, cautiously creeping over fascinating slabs of rock and boulder. In time, as he slowly inched along, Adam could almost see a glimpse of a white, Nordic sky where the light seeped through on the sides. When he finally reached the mouth of the cave, Adam stood still, witnessing an awesome sight – the beauteous waking of Iceland.

"Much to take in," the recognizable voice of the king whispered. Adam turned his head slightly then fully faced his host and said, "We often take things for granted." Teitur breathed once again and lifted his eyes to peer through the wide opening from which the glorious light was coming. "True ....this is true......," he continued now nodding slowly; "but not this....no – this would be a crime to overlook." Adam silently agreed with this exceedingly true statement, as they both stood watching Krafla Springs come to life.

"I need to find out who I am," Adam stated quietly after a moment of staring off into the distance. Another wave of silence flooded the dry atmosphere.

"I know who you are." He closed his eyes and tilted his head back inhaling the glacial air. "My job as king is to watch over every troll, know them in every way, even if they don't know themselves," the wise troll added.

"So then you can tell me." Adam stared up in belief, gazing at the aging crown atop the king's head. The troll king, with his eyes closed, exhaled a wondrous sigh.

"Not quite. Did you fail to hear yesterday of the momentous tasks of our ancestors before us. Unlike the foolishness and waste that Gryla's tale holds, they suffered for us in honor so that we may follow, yet make our own story." He paused and looked down on Adam who was now recanting the legend of the trolls - "In this honor I decide to watch all, respect all yet let all decide and discover for themselves." With this, the troll king nodded and turned his back to the light.

"Well," Adam cried loudly to his own surprise and dismay. He then lowered his voice and asked, "......can't you at least help me in any way?......Please," he whispered. Without looking directly at him, the king responded, "Hvitserkur" and walked away unaccompanied.

Adam found himself in awe, once again where he had started at the mouth of the cave. He was alone once more to assess his knowledge; whispering "Hvitserkur ….. White Rock".

END OF BOOK TWO - JP

ALTERNATIVE BOOK TWO: SGP

OR "A few feet away from the intruders, the troll spoke in a booming, gravelly voice. "My name is Teitur. I am King of the Trolls. Welcome to our cave.""

For every beginning, there is an ending. And, of course, with every ending, something new begins.

Teitur, King of the Trolls, a lanky, noble creature, knew he was standing on that fragile precipice, the thin, jagged line between that which is as it becomes what was. It is what we call the present, the place in which most trolls eternally exist.

Teitur knew this with an unusual sense of clarity, for trolls, even kings, are changeable beasts, both in their necessary daylight change to stone and in their relative inability to think long-term. Trolls are notoriously wishy-washy. The constant need to change into and out of stone had affected not only their limbs, but their brains' ability to form thoughts fluidly.

People thought trolls ferocious, when in reality their ferocity was merely the outward expression of the effort it took to form thoughts, or come to conclusions – to pull any words or actions or choices from the middle of their hoary troll minds.

(An aside for the doubting reader – evidence of this reality abounds in this very scene, for why would the parade of trolls stomp past the cave when Adam and Freyr had taken a left into it before their very eyes. Or explore the smell in the cave where we find ourselves... a blend of rot and fester. Few know that trolls' teeth are so gruesome because they forget to brush them. And to try to explain the long-term consequences of poor dental hygiene is useless as it would require planning and forethought and they would forget, and once their teeth were rotten there was no sense in crying over spilt milk. Trolls hate milk. Finally, and perhaps the best example of a troll's lack of foresight, is Gryla's choice to turn herself into stone so she could live forever and now she lives not much of a life, standing as a giant stone off the shore of the stormy ocean.)

So Teitur stood staring at the lanky elf and his new-found pal, Freyr. The trolls stared too. None of them questioned the king's ability to use his brain, trolls being trolls, living mostly in the moment. They were used to standing still, waiting for nothing in particular.

"What is it you want?" Teitur finally roared.

Adam flinched at the thunderous sound; Freyr, a human used to choosing from aisles of breath-freshening, tooth preservation products pinched his nose and said "eeeewww."

Adam knew it had been a mistake to bring the boy. He gave him a quick poke in the ribs.

"Hey," Freyr whined.

"Well, Sir," Adam stuttered. "I have been sent by Fladnag, the great and powerful wizard who is currently in residence at the Hotel Reykjavik."

The crowd of trolls behind the king scratched their heads, muttering that the name and place sounded familiar, though none could really place either. Teitur, however, had no problem calling up in his mind the face of the famed wizard, nor Reykjavik, for it was on the outskirts of the town where he'd spent his childhood. And, as mentioned, Teitur had a good mind.

"And for what reason has the Great Fladnag sent you here to seek us among the land of geysers and volcanoes. If he is great and powerful and wise, why would he send you to the feet of your enemies. For you are an elf, albeit a lanky one, are you not?"

"Well sir, that's the thing of it," Adam said, speaking as loudly as he could. This another misconception, that trolls roar to display their ferocious might. Knowing now the true story behind their ferocity, it will make sense to you dear reader, that they simply roar because of the amount of hair in their ears. Adam had a good deal of hair in his own big ears, which now that he knew he was of troll descent, he had to say made sense – both their size, shape and hairiness were quite different than his elf brethren. "I'm not an enemy. I'm one of you. At least that's what Fladnag says."

The trolls surrounding King Teitur, Freyr and Adam snickered and whispered to one another, clearly thinking Adam, whom they believed to be an elf, had lost his mind. Teitur, however, gazed at Adam steadily, as if willing him to recognize something. Adam stared back into eyes that were strangely familiar.

"You have not answered my question. I did not ask if you believe yourself to be foe or friend, but rather for what reason does Fladnag send you?" Teitur thundered.

"To unite species – to unite the trolls and hidden folk," Adam said, ducking a bit when he finished the words for he totally expected the king to whack his head for uttering such a silly mission.

Instead, Teitur surprised him. "Very interesting. Very interesting indeed. And did the Great Fladnag say why he thought you among the many could accomplish this task?"

"Uh, no" Adam admitted, cursing himself for not pausing to wonder this himself – uck, another sign of trollishness.

"Well, let me tell you a tale," Teitur said, sweeping his powerful, gnarly arms out wide. The gesture was clearly a familiar one to the trolls, who plopped down grinning great grins of pleasure. "We wuv stories," the troll next to Adam and Freyr confessed.

Slowly, dramatically, with incredible panache the king told the tale of Gryla and her cheating husband Leppa-Ludi. He spoke of how the feckless Leppa-Ludi cheated on his wife with the elf Skjoda; and how Gryla punished them all, and how her sons, still alive have hunted the hidden folk ever since.

"Yes. I know the tale," Adam said, a bit impatiently.

"Well I've never heard the story," Freyr said. "But we Icelanders do know of the hidden folk and of the trolls hidden in stone. More people believe than anywhere else in the world. We believe in what we cannot see."

Another attribute necessary for being a king is patience, and Teitur was a patient troll. He had to be - living with the messy, stinky forgetful mob that he did.

"There is a part of the tale that was never told, for when Gryla turned Skjoda and her family to stone, one child remained – a dwarf. For that is what you get when you cross an elf and a troll."

A stunned silence fell over the listeners – or at least for Adam it was a moment of stunned silence – with trolls it 's difficult to tell if you've surprised them, or if they've simply forgotten what you've said and they're waiting for more.

"And because the child was a dwarf," Adam spoke his thoughts aloud: "Gryla's curse never worked."

Teitur slowly nodded, giving Adam a smile that spoke volumes about his respect for the lanky youngster.

"Yes. The dwarf-child, a girl, went on to marry and have children of her own." Teitur said. "And because she married a troll, the children were oddly enough, lanky. You see, if a troll marries a dwarf, the children are lanky. If a dwarf marries an elf, the children are squat. It's how the genetics of the hidden world work."

Suddenly, Adam realized what was familiar. Teitur had his same lanky build, his same amber eyes. Teitur looked a good deal like him.

Are we??" Adam left the thought unfinished, but Teitur understood.

"Yes. We are related," the King said. "Your mother was my sister. She chose to call herself an elf. I chose to remain with the trolls. As you know, your mother died when she failed to hide herself before the sun rose one morning. The elves who raised you, may or may not have known the truth. Being wholly elf, they would have hidden it if they did.

"And so now it is your task to return to your world. To encourage your brethren to believe peace is possible," Teitur commanded (to be honest, Adam was getting tired of wizards and kings bossing him around). "And I will try to do the same here. I have been trying for these many years. However, Gryla seems to have etched in the trolls' stony minds a hatred for elves. It seems to be the one thing they remember."

"Trolls hate people," Freyr interrupted.

"Ah, not so young boy," the King said. "People believe the trolls hate them, because people think trolls are different and look scary. But it has never been a troll's desire to scare young children, as the story goes."

"Oh," Freyr breathed with understanding.

"And, so, as I was saying: go forth Adam, to unite our worlds."

"Okay," Adam said, turning slowly toward the mouth of the cave, already pondering how he would tackle such an immense mission.

Freyr followed him, piping up that he would help if he could.

"Thanks," Adam said.

And so ends Book Two. But remember, in every ending is a beginning.

END OF BOOK TWO - SGP

ABOUT THE AUTHOR

Residing on Cape Cod, Massachusetts. HaiDi Pye currently attends Nauset Regional High School.   Her primary interests include art, photography and reading.

Although writing fiction was never an aspiration of hers, HaiDi at age thirteen wrote Book One for her grandmother as a birthday gift, promising sequels to follow shortly. The following year, she invited her mother, sister, aunt and cousin to each create their own endings, along with her. Presenting five versions of Book Two, HaiDi and her co-writers brought diverse stories to the birthday celebration, reading aloud their works. Each introduced new ideas and thoughts on what happened after the original story, which eventually led to the creation of the "Elves, Trolls & Cheese Curls – a Tale of Icelandic Creatures" short series.

Made in the USA
Charleston, SC
16 November 2015